S0-FUM-962

The Star Traveler

... A Journey of the Spirit ...

by Dr. Ilse-Maria Fahrnow

Copyright © 2006 by Viamar International Inc.

All rights reserved. No part of this book may be reproduced or utilized in any form or by any means, electronic or mechanical, including photocopying, recording or by any information storage or retrieval system, without permission in writing from the Publisher.

Text by Dr. Ilse-Maria Fahrnow
Illustrated by Jürgen Fahrnow
www.alleelemente.de

Translated from German by Roselle Nordtome
www.nordtome.com

Book Layout and Publishing by Marita Mitschein, Viamar International Inc.
www.maritamitschein.com

Library of Congress Cataloging-in-Publication Data
is available from the Library of Congress.

ISBN 978-0-9789757-5-3

Printed in the United States of America

Epilogue

This story tells of seemingly unbelievable things that carry the impact of a utopian fable. Many of these previously unused human potentials, e.g. telepathy, do however exist; albeit we do not exactly understand it. Psychological research suggests that we humans, at best, are only familiar with and use 10% of our potential. We use unconscious perceptions to navigate through our lives to a great degree. We limit our actual opportunities with prejudice and rigid beliefs; and yet our learning capacity is much greater than we can even estimate at this time.

In the beginning of this new millennium, we are all invited to create our ideal world intentionally and responsibly. There are many well thought out concepts already in place to support the model of the "Healing Temple", and there are many people who want to participate in its realization. Perhaps we will meet in this context some day? In any case, Dear Reader, we wish you heartfelt success in your deepest desires and hopes! May you be supported by the light and the message from the green dog!

Yours,

Dr. Ilse-Maria and Jürgen Fahrnow,
Marita Mitschein and Roselle Nordtome

Prologue

Traveler through the worlds of the divine Universe – anchored and rooted within the inner temple of divine wisdom – regenerated, transformed and enlightened in the Healing Temple – connected to the sounds and colors of creation – enveloped and interlaced with the ONE BEING: I AM THAT I AM!

"Don't believe the fairy tales – they are true"
Polish Saying

1

Stop – there it is again: the vibrant, glowing light of the stars above him! Or does this all just live inside him? Rocco's body feels light and heavy at the same time. A pulsing rhythm flows through him head to toe. It is 2:30 am, and he sits upright abruptly in his bed. The dream that just led him on a journey through the glimmering vastness of the universe shatters into millions of fiery sparks. Rocco reaches out to these sparks, trying to fit the image back together. Yet everything that was just his is dissolved and lost. Disappointed, Rocco sighs and stretches out again on his bed. Why, oh why is it so difficult to hold and comprehend the wonders he encounters on his dream journeys?

Rocco knows this dream and loves it. In countless variations he traverses the worlds beyond his everyday world. Often, he feels insights or messages seep into his consciousness. How he would LOVE to gather and keep them … Yet in the moment of his awakening, they all scatter to be lost forever.
„What is part of you can never be lost" Rocco hears a soft voice inside.
'Oh dear,' thinks Rocco, he hears voices … is he beginning to go insane?

The Star Traveler

"Quite the opposite! When you perceive this truth, you put the world back in order! Insane is to think that anything in this universe could be lost!"

"Who is talking to me?" asks Rocco into the dark of his bedroom and listens intently, but, except for the tinkling sound of laughter, bright as a silver bell, there is nothing to hear (or is it only the sound of the little wind chime in the garden?).

All of us wander through our lives, navigating the inner and outer realms of our Being. Some proceed with continuous dedication, others engage in stop-and-go. A part of us burdens itself with baggage; another steps forward lightly. And most of us are on a path of searching. Something drives us on relentlessly. Something whispers to us the essence of life: It goes on!

This story lets us share with someone who widely expands his travels. He scouts not only the regions of his home planet. Rocco is driven into the vastness of his unlimited Being. Faint flashing lights on velvety-black background – there his longing lives.

As far back as he can think – and this is indeed far back, thousands of years – he dreams in his

The Star Traveler

sleep of wandering through the expanse of the Universe. This dream always begins the same way: Rocco lays spread out upon a meadow, soft as velvet and yet firmly supported, and gazes into the night sky above him. As his body relaxes, his spirit begins to travel. The blinking stars above him invite him to be their guest. With the swiftness of a thought, he is already moving: on the way to his personal journey to the stars, full of excitement and joy in his heart, a pioneer on the way into Infinity.

Each star is something special: Divine Beings who yield their all, blazing fires who surrender without hesitation – melting, redeeming. On his home planet, Rocco experiences the duality: day and night, light and shadow, warmth and cold. As his planet faces the sun and then revolves into the dark, so evolves a world of conflict in which only one of his multiple potentials becomes manifest. This is the secret of the Receivers.

But a star – a star's life is a gift in itself. Without pause, in a constant dance of elements, fiery, explosive and full of light, the star gives of itself. Without judgment it gifts all of creation with itself. This is what attracts Rocco like a magnet. He will travel there, to explore the laws of life. He is not yet aware that what drives him to the

The Star Traveler

journey is his inner soul. The soul is part of the divine fire. It lives according to the laws of the stars. It surrenders itself in love and holds nothing back. So it MOVES Rocco onto the path. The soul desires insight.
It wants to experience unification with the heavenly fires of its divine home. And, of course, it desires unification with Rocco. Thus it draws him.

Rocco feels this drawing like a sweet longing in his breast, and this longing is usually so strong that it awakens him. Then he lays, thinking for a while beneath the firmament, contemplating the glittering infinity and pondering on how this longing in his life can find fulfillment. And this is the beginning of our story

The Star Traveler

2

Rocco wakes to the sound of streaming rain. "I might as well just go back to sleep", he thinks. It is Sunday, so there's nothing really important to do. During the week, Rocco works at a school for special kids. "Handicapped", they are called, because they do not learn with the same rhythm as most others. They are, so to speak, outside the norm. For Rocco, they are very special Beings – especially talented and especially giving. They often offer him impressions and ideas that make his inner soul gleeful. The soul is gleeful, because, whether 'handicapped' or 'normal', the soul knows and loves all other souls. It knows that all are made of the same fabric.

Rocco's children are star travelers just like he is. Only, they allow themselves to step out any time they feel like it. While they sit in their wheelchairs, leaving school assignments to wilt on their own, their spirits roam and explore the whole picture of life. Naturally, the small segment called school gets short-changed. So what? A handicap can open room for new adventures.
Now, it is Sunday.
The kids are at home and gift their families with their own special talents.

The Star Traveler

Rocco is off work. Softly, his spirit expands, and the journey begins.

Rocco drifts, feeling wonderfully light in his body, out into the All.

The light here is intensely bright and colorful, different from how one could imagine it from the Earth.

Rocco passes through a nebula of golden, glimmering dust clouds. They enfold and suffuse him.

Right here, he feels how the consciousness of the nebula converges with his own.

Suddenly he realizes how he shimmers with the nebula's golden light.

Could it, should it be so easy to unite?

"When you surrender, everything is easy", the voice inside whispers.

'Well, if it's like this, I want more of it' Rocco thinks – and immediately, the golden cloud vanishes from his awareness.

"That's not fair" he just manages to think – and doesn't realize that his greed engenders a new dynamic. How, after all, could he understand that his various ego-powered emotions can create so many different environments?

Rocco however is on his path of enjoyment and learning; hence he will not be stopped now. He also knows with more certainty what he seeks: more of this wonderful light feeling of golden unity. That is what draws him. The stars seem to possess it. They sparkle golden and flow without pause.

Rocco allows his awareness to drift. Actually, he does not know that it is his awareness which is drifting. He has not yet scouted out the multilevel forms of his Being.

He is simply enjoying the floating. His body feels light, and all thoughts have become unimportant.

Thus he meets the star master of Sirius. He knows this feeling from his dreams: suddenly he senses a great, powerful presence. Awe captures him. Then his whole essence is flooded with clarity and limitless love. Again he feels unification. A wave of happiness permeates him.

Sirius – blue white star at the perimeter of our visible universe. Now that Rocco is here, he recognizes the narrow limits of the earthly field of vision. Here, all limits have dissolved. Infinite, bright expanse fills all that is. Rocco himself feels limitless and wide. At the same time he is connected with all that is. Thus he can hear the star master's voice inside himself. Stop – is that possible? "Inside himself?"

Very clearly, Rocco perceives a voice. He even separates words and sounds when he listens closely. But, where are these words? Where do they come from? In this moment, Rocco has no answer to his questions. Everything, at the same time, seems right. So, he lets his questions rest and listens.

"Thank you" says his heart. And "we love you" the answer comes. Now, what is all that about? Who is "we"?
"The developed awareness that each *I* a part of a *WE*" says the star master now.
Ah – Rocco knows this voice. This sound is familiar to him. Rocco trusts the star master. This is because they have known each other for so very long. Rocco digs in the caverns of his memory and finds neither beginning nor end to this friendship. It feels as though the star master has always been with him – in him? "Yes" says the star master presently "you are on the right track, Rocco. We have always been ONE. You are – we are – the multiplicity of the ONE BEING!"

Now Rocco's reasonable mind begins to balk. As much as Rocco enjoys these meetings with the star master – some times these universal sages just go too far. How can a normal human being understand these dichotomies? Rocco just wants to shut down.
Then he hears the star master again: "Let your mind rest a while, dear brother. Your mind is subject to the laws of the three-dimensional

universe. It knows time as a string and the arrangement of Beings in boxes. Moreover, it is trained to decide immediately what is right and wrong. Thus you have created it and thus it works. It is your machine, your tool! It can only do what you have enabled it to do. So, please: do not expect your mind to understand greater connections. Install a few new programs which will enable it to grasp life with more complicated structures if you want to give it such tasks!"

While Rocco listens to these words, his mind mutters softly to itself. It feels criticized and unjustly judged. Every day, it gives its best to make life easier for Rocco – and then some stranger comes along who wants to change all that . . . Rocco's mind hopes that his master won't linger too long on this subject. ..

However, Rocco's soul desires vitality. It shakes and vibrates impatiently, eager to enter into the vaster realms of the universe. It twitches and pulls inside – so much that Rocco submits to its longing. Already, a channel is opened, and the star master's words are once more flowing into his consciousness.

"Life is about Balance, dear Rocco" he is saying. "This is difficult for you, on your planet of opposites. Your world is always partially in the dark and partially in the light. Moreover, while one part of you is in the light, other people on

The Star Traveler

earth are in the dark. Light and shadow are constantly changing. Therefore your perception is challenged to the utmost. What is in the light for some is simultaneously in the dark for others. You are in opposition – even amongst yourselves - difficult for you – really not easy!"

Rocco understands immediately what is said. "But why are we making it so difficult? How can we make it easier?" he asks the star master. Then he feels a jolt, and already he is in the midst of the glowing, lavish power of light.
Rocco looks down on his body: everything seems to consist of explosive, vibrating, infinitely fast moving particles. He himself is perfect light!
"You see" he hears the star master say "This is the reality! You are the reality!"
In this moment, Rocco feels as light as every one of these sparks of light that make up his Being. He is light – and life is levity!
"Why does that work all of a sudden?" his mind wants to know. "Why do I otherwise feel so heavy in life?" These two questions were apparently enough to make Rocco's glimmering glowing star body dense and heavy again.
Suddenly, he notices that he is lying in bed. It is Sunday morning; rain is pouring down – and Rocco feels infinitely heavy and tired.

The Star Traveler

3

The week passes quickly. Rocco goes to school and enjoys his time with his ‚special' kids. Every so often, a child's gaze hits him right in the middle of his heart. Then he feels it again: this longing twitching and pulling inside. Do the children know of this? The ones who are the most distant sometimes seem to be right there. Rocco finds his life confusing. On top of all this, he must now write an assessment for the kids. How on earth can he judge young people who obviously live under totally different premises than those offered on the assessment forms? Rocco does not know what to do and is glad that the weekend is drawing near again – time for him to dream and travel.

This time, the sun is laughing in the sky. Rocco stuffs some food and drinks into his back pack and takes off: out into nature! To rest on a wonderful meadow; close to the body of this planet he loves so much!

Just as Rocco wants to take a little nap, his legs begin to itch: the ants are building a detour for their highway. He has placed himself just over their path without noticing. He, the giant, is even covering up the dead beetle they want to transport into their pile. Well, they must sting a little now – their ant acid helps. Rocco sits up and complains: whose planet is this, anyway? Well, somehow the issue seems to be co-existence – or maybe dominance? Who rules whom here?

Suddenly, he feels again the familiar stream of light as it flows through his body – as though someone had flipped a switch (maybe this actually happens before light appears? Who, however, is the one who flips the switch?) – As though someone HAD flipped a switch, Rocco feels himself as ONE with the ants and the rest of the world. At the same moment, he knows that a few feet away there is a wonderful, ant-free little spot for him: HIS spot in the meadow! Here, he interrupts no one, and therefore he is uninterrupted. Here is harmony – and his body glows again.

Somehow, though, the afternoon sun must have made him sleepy. How else could a green dog suddenly sit in front of him? "Dogs are black, white, brown, or maybe tan" his mind immediately and sternly comments. Perhaps it is because of the bright sunlight that has let red blots dance in front of his eyes all this time? Maybe his ocular nerves have magically created the complementary color green? While Rocco is still searching for a plausible explanation for the green dog, a hot wave of joy suddenly flows through him. He feels so light and happy that he would love to embrace the whole world. Is it illusion or did the green dog just speak to him?

"See – this joyful feeling is a beautiful gift from your heart to you! Does my green color puzzle you? Green is the love vibration of the heart. The freer and purer your heart's power can flow, the more green hues will show in your aura. Where I come from, all Beings live out of the power of love. We have all discovered this power. We nurture and protect it like a precious possession. Love comes directly from the source of Creation. Once you know it, you will want more and more of it. You humans are still settling for a very small portion of love. Don't be so modest! Allow yourselves more of it!"

'More love' Rocco thinks – 'ah that would be nice!' How he yearns to have a mate who gives him love – and how he would give himself totally in love; strange – while he harbors these thoughts, the dog's green color begins to flicker and fluoresce. It looks as though a part of this energy wants to flow towards him.
Rocco suddenly feels strangely hard and closed up; and the green wave makes a detour and flows away from him. With it, the light feeling of joy disappears. Pensively, the green dog looks

The Star Traveler

at Rocco. "Why do you not accept what wants to join you?" he seems to ask.

Rocco rubs his eyes and blinks. Apparently he really did doze off. Nature all around him shines in summery green, the colors of a thousand blossoms woven in. Farther away, two girls stroll across the meadow and giggle unabashedly. 'Rocco – that means rock?' Rocco ponders. How can a rock become light and flowing? He feels something skip in his chest. He looks after the girls and feels strangely relaxed, contented. Strengthened and light-footed, he begins his journey home.

4

Monday morning – the week begins.

"You have seen the green dog!" says Nina as Rocco enters the class room.

Nina can speak? Rocco must be mistaken. This little girl is unable to speak?! Nina has lived with this handicap since birth; it allows no speech to grow in her. At least, this remark is in her school records …

Rocco must have made a mistake. Yet, just as he wants to turn around, he hears her loud and clear: "Has he told you about love, too? You see, that's his favorite subject – teehee – love – favorite subject …!" Rocco jerks around to look at Nina. Her whole face beams as she claps her hands.

"What do you know of the green dog?" he asks her. Nina only laughs and starts making spitballs with her lips. He must have misheard.

Yet, this Monday morning is full of surprises. Every time Rocco wants to start his 'normal' day in school, something confusing happens.

Now Peter interrupts. Peter has a spastic paralysis. His muscles do as they please, and Peter is usually entirely subject to their uncontrolled movements. In this moment, however, he points a very calm finger towards Nina, then towards Rocco, and then a coltish laughter erupts from him. "He doesn't know that you know . . ." Peter manages between two attacks of laughter.

Right then, all the children explode in jaunty laughter. Not only that, but they find it most entertaining to emit all sorts of funny noises. The class room turns into an orchestra of joy.
"I sure hope the dean won't stop by right now" Rocco just manages to think before his mind suddenly feels light and empty, as though a whirlwind had swept through it. Rollicking like a child, he joins the happy laughter. In the process, his heart beings to warm – and although he has no idea from where this comes, Rocco notices a mild, green light that permeates the whole class room.

"That was a strange day" Rocco thinks as he goes home at dusk. As is his habit, he looks up to the heavens. His mind is somewhat nervous about the carefree escapades he allows himself, but Rocco recognizes without doubt that the wonderful, shining evening star is winking at him personally. His heart just knows it!
"This is Venus, and we live here! Discover more love within you, humans, and we will meet more often!"
Was this just the voice of the green dog?

The Star Traveler

"Of course" he hears Nina say. Abruptly, Rocco turns around – and discovers himself all alone on the street.

'Maybe I must get used to hearing voices. As long as the conversations are interesting, it can be a lot of fun' Rocco thinks. "We are all connected" he hears Nina's fair voice within himself. "Of course, everyone decides if and when he will open his hearing".
Pensively, Rocco saunters home. 'If that is really true, then I am never alone' the thoughts pass through his head; and without knowing why, he suddenly feels nicely warm and well protected.

The Star Traveler

5

With the levity of a dreamer, he soon drifts through the spiraling whirls of light in the Milky Way. A truly divine view offers itself: everywhere, the diamond dust clouds of stars twinkle and glitter. All even remotely thinkable colors waft into geometric patterns. These patterns are themselves engaged in constant change. Everything lives and weaves, moves, transforms itself – in an endless dance of divine creation. Deep amazement captures Rocco. Full of awe, he observes this multiplicity of pure light.

A slight drawing sensation in his chest lets him know to follow an invitation. His soul has fashioned a tryst for him. He knows not, yet, where this will lead him – but he knows the feeling of invitation well. He also knows the consequence of ignoring the invitation of his soul. This state is uncomfortable within – like a too-small shirt. Soon he cannot move freely and comfortably. The inner constriction has a tendency to spread itself everywhere – and the wonderful, glowing inner flow that he loves so much begins to trickle away. Finally it stops completely. Then he feels stiff, crabby, moody, uneasy, and irritable. This is really a very uncomfortable state.

The Star Traveler

Thus it is always advisable to follow the invitations of his soul – even if he doesn't know where the journey leads.

"Trust me" says his soul. And: "Have I ever betrayed you?" Rocco agrees with his soul. It may lead him on extraordinary ways, but ultimate joy and bliss are the outcome of all its actions. To follow his soul is usually the simplest way. So Rocco exhales softly, and already he is gliding on – without giving another thought to the direction of his travel.

In the blink of an eye he has already arrived. He feels his body's motion stopping. Apparently he has landed on a planet, for the floating lightness of his body has given way to a certain gravity. Around him, he sees ochre sand, a sort of dry desert. Rocco tries a few steps to find out how best to move here. In the process he notices that his thoughts are immediately turned into actions.

He would like to climb a small hill – as soon as he thinks it, he is already on top. "Oops", Rocco thinks "I must be careful what I think!" A fleeting thought of Nina places her – right here! She sits in her wheelchair in the midst of the dire, dry landscape of this planet. She offers an impish laugh, turns three circles, wheel chair and all, and – poof – is gone again.

The Star Traveler

"I can do that, too" he just hears her say "My thoughts, too, turn into motion!"
Is she part of the assignation his soul has made for him?

"You have just learned" his wise soul whisper to him "That you can never be alone, for you are connected with all that is. I will show you now the entire greatness of this reality. Please open the chamber of your heart. Let this room expand. Let it become greater and greater … and now enfold therein all that has ever happened to you. Invite all of creation to find a home in your heart. Can you feel how you are ever expanding? Do you feel the wonderful abundance within? Can you feel how this goes on and on?"

Rocco marvels, amazed. The endless expanse of his Inner Self feels soft and cozy. He is rich – yet modest and simple at once. Endless vastness, endless, multiplex abundance – and all that exists in the dot of a single Being.
His Being! Quiet, calm, self confidence and pride begin to spread within him. Suddenly he feels the proximity of the green dog and deep love flows through him. With great clarity – clear as the sun and the stars – he knows that love is the greatest of all powers. Universes move and

universes rest – according to the impulses of this power!

"Well done, Rocco" whispers his soul "Now you have understood something really important! When you see the green dog you recognize the essence of love!"
So his special school children have recognized the essence of love? His special 'handicapped' children? Their silver bright, joyful laughter still sounds in him. A new hunch arises in his awareness: should one not see the whole world with new eyes? A soft buzzing trails through his head. It sounds as though hundreds of tiny angels were applauding. "Right" they whisper excitedly "Look at the world with eyes of love and re-create your new Self!" Now, Rocco feels how his inner stiffness begins to softly melt.

The Star Traveler

6

All the school children are excited when Rocco comes to class the next morning. They look at him with eager faces. "Did you get to know all the others yet?" asks little Alexander who usually just sits still in a corner.

"No" interrupts Nina "he's only been on one Jupiter planet. After all, he must first learn something of the abundance; but I think he did well with his exercises."

"Did he understand the essence of love?" another little girl asks excitedly.

Rocco is moved and confused. Why do these kids worry so about him?

Apparently, they heard his inner question, for right away one answers: "You are an adult, and a teacher to boot. It is important that you learn to understand the essence of love. Ultimately, you'd like to live in peace, right?"

Rocco does not know anymore how he should answer. His whole world has gone topsy-turvy. He is the teacher, and quite matter-of-factly, he is receiving lessons from his handicapped school children. Has he unknowingly gone crazy after all? Or, is he still lying in bed, just dreaming that his day has begun?

The Star Traveler

While Rocco indulges his thoughts, the children keep debating excitedly

"He must meet the monkey" says Peter "that would make him laugh a little."

"And, the trip to the water planet is important, too, so he can get a little more fluid" another boy chimes in.

"He can already fly, but a meeting with the birds could give him new input" a thin, quiet girl volunteers.

'Is anyone going to ask MY opinion?' Rocco thinks quietly.

"But, of course!" cries a boy from the back bench. "Without your OK nothing can happen!" Rocco is feeling more and more embarrassed. He cannot even think privately anymore ….

"Don't let it bother you" Nina chirps "better get used to telepathy right away. It is a practical way to communicate, anyway. Besides, there is nothing you have to hide. We are all in the same boat …"

The star master has often pointed out that all of creation is ONE on a deeper level. Until now, Rocco has benevolently accepted these 'sayings' and then filed them away in his inner drawer of 'philosophy'. Today's events keep confusing him over and over. How much of this is philosophy, and how much is reality? How shall he navigate through these ever-changing experiences?

"Just let the classification go" says a familiar voice in him. Rocco sighs with relief.

The star master is here – his ancient friend from Sirius. Hopefully, he can, with his quiet nature, bring order into Rocco's chaos.

"Philosophy or reality – you KNOW that life does not follow classifications" the star master says now.

"All that counts is only you! With your perception you create your reality! And it is then valid! Therefore love is so significant. Let your perception flow through a filter of love, and thus create a loving world!"

'Sounds temptingly simple' Rocco thinks 'but how, if you please, does this work in daily life? How and where do I begin?'

In this moment, his soul speaks up and grants him a soft, relaxing breath of hope.

"Let the many thoughts come to rest, dearest Rocco" it whispers to him. "You understand simply as you experience! Life is so much greater than all the words you know; and the most important insights flow into your awareness while by-passing the words, anyway. Rest a while, and look forward to your next star

The Star Traveler

journey – soon, everything will make more sense!"

Rocco looks up – and into the expectant faces of his kids. Ah yes, of course – they probably heard everything, didn't they? Peter's soft nod shows him that there is nothing else to be said.
"Will you come with me on my next journey?" he asks them. Their smiles are his answer. "You really still have a lot to learn" Nina bursts out – "we're already here!"

The Star Traveler

7

Rocco is sad without knowing why. A wistful mood has spread in him. He feels strangely 'un-alive' and cut off.

"Cut off – from what?" a quiet voice within him asks. "How would you separate, in this universe, from all that is? How should one drop in the ocean separate from all the rest of the water?"

"Real simple" Rocco's reason volunteers "If the drop knows that it is a drop, it is immediately sectioned off"

'Great' Rocco thinks; 'Does IT intermingle now, too?' Up to now he could at least trust his reason to offer clear lines to sort out the chaos. "What a strange statement is that? If the drop knows that it is a drop … that would mean …"

"Bingo!" he hears the children giggle and clap. They clap their hands and are frisky with joy. But, he is sitting at home in his room. Can he have no peace by himself anywhere?

"But yes, of course you can" he hears Nina warble. Nina – the one who allegedly cannot speak. How does this all fit? For now, she speaks quite clearly; even when she isn't even in the same room.

"But I am! We are all in your room! In your inner room! You know how they say 'as inside so outside' – recognize that, teacher? By the way, you can turn us off if you've had enough".

"And how does that work?" Rocco asks.

"Just think of something else – poof – we're gone! We can only be with you when you give us your attention …"

Aha – it's like that! His consciousness seems to have a great influence upon these events. Can he likewise also control what happens?

"If the drop knows that it is a drop … do we create our limits only within ourselves?" Rocco ponders. "And, what does all that have to do with knowing oneself? If the drop knows that it is a drop, does it then also know WHO it is? Does it know itself?" Rocco finds these mental exercises tiring. He doesn't really know why his reason has started up this carousel of thought.

He must have gone to sleep; or, is he experiencing a sort of waking dream? In any case, he suddenly feels wonderfully light and connected. There is movement in him and around him – like a very soft rocking and gliding. All sadness has melted away. Yes – to be precise, he doesn't even know any more how it felt.

"I thought so. It is good for him to be more fluid" the little boy from the class room just says. His channel to the children must still be open.

But, he must agree with the boy – somehow he feels very warm, flowing and lively. All around

The Star Traveler

him, everything seems to flow as well. Has he landed on the water planet? Rocco definitely enjoys this situation. Everything in him relaxes. He is quiet, contented and happy.

"Does the drop know, then, that it is a drop?" Immediately the pleasant movement halts, and Rocco feels wide awake.
"To be separate, to be connected - there must be a way to be consciously connected with all that is? That would mean that the drop knows it is a drop – and at the same time, it knows that it is part of the ocean; and he knows that this ocean consists of innumerable other drops that all also belong to the whole. Yes – they all together make up the whole!"
Rocco's consciousness distends and stretches itself. He almost thinks he can hear a soft popping noise in his chest. Suddenly, everything fits together: Rocco experiences, in the expanded rooms of his Being, that all these single insights are of equal and parallel value.

"Good work" the soft voice from before whispers. "Dearest Rocco, you are rounding out and maturing every day. Your aura twinkles and shines; every time you have understood another of the laws of wisdom of life. We rejoice with you and congratulate you!"

The Star Traveler

There, in the corner of his room Rocco notices a glowing, shining figure. As he looks closer, he recognizes a beautiful little sea horse. Its ancient form is created according to the laws of geometry.

"What wonders this universe brings" Rocco thinks.

8

Rocco is called in to see the dean. With a queasy feeling in his belly he enters the dean's room and closes the door behind him. This must certainly be trouble … The dean looks long and inquiringly into Rocco's eyes.

"Strange things are being reported about you lately" he begins. "It is nice of you to spread cheerfulness in the class room. Still, especially these handicapped children desperately need a reliable, quiet order. We must teach them structure and coordination. This is their only chance of finding a good place later on in their real lives."

"You mean this is not real life?" Rocco would love to ask, but he thinks it is smarter to keep this comment to him.

Besides, the dean already continues: "Please keep in mind that these children come from quite normal, socially integrated families. Most of them also have normal siblings. There is little understanding for travels and jokes.

"How does he know …?" Rocco ponders quietly. He can hardly follow the dean's words. His head feels strangely foggy. "It's not all that simple" he wants to say. "Normal children, handicapped children, a real life, and unreal life … who will classify all that correctly …?"

The Star Traveler

"By the way, Nina can speak", he says, glad for his ability to contribute to this odd conversation. The dean wrinkles his forehead. For a moment he seems to assess whether or not Rocco is truly still normal.

"You must be wrong here" he then says with conviction. "That is totally impossible with this child's diagnosis".

Rocco sighs. The situation seems impossible. How can he explain all the many, sometimes unspeakable levels through which he has traveled recently to the dean?

'It should be possible for one drop to speak to another' he thinks. Carefully, he looks into the dean's eyes and smiles a little.

And, suddenly, the green dog is in the room. Very quietly it sits there and exudes its mild, green light. Now Rocco knows without a doubt that the dean has a heart full of love in his chest. Therefore it is now totally unimportant to him whether or not the dean can see the green dog.

Where a loving heart beats, all other things are unimportant!

The dean loves the children! He also loves him! His strong critique has grown on the soil of good intention and caring love. 'Then all is well' Rocco thinks.

Truly, the atmosphere in the room has changed. The dean looks at him kindly.

"Just see to it that the children learn to differentiate between fun and business" he says. "We must be a little careful. The schools inspector holds a tight rein, and I don't want her to disturb our work."

Even though Rocco has no idea how to teach the children the difference between fun and business, he is very glad that this uncomfortable conversation is coming to a good end at last. He puts off the difference between fun and business for later – for that is something he has to think about for himself first.

The Star Traveler

9

Softly, Rocco drifts through the glittering, secretive vastness of the universe. He knows and loves this feeling: carried on a steadily flowing movement, secure and warmly protected in the rooms of his inner wisdom, he floats through his universe in the eternal light of creation. All is well as it is.

Constant transformation and metamorphosis create the patterns and structures of planets and stars. Each star a hot fire of divine love that illuminates everything; warms and permeates all existence. Each planet a vessel turned into shape which receives and passes on these currents.

Rocco loves them all. Without words, he understands the WHOLE secret of creation. Simultaneously joined and spread out are the myriads of divine sparks: drops in the ocean of love! Unique personalities as well as parts of a collective soul at the same time. What a delicious feeling to be part of it!

While Rocco glides on, he notices that he is riding on a great, soft wing. Fine feathers carry him; decorated with patterns of red pearl all around him. The pearl eagle has picked him up to make his journey more comfortable. Rocco

The Star Traveler

cannot pinpoint the moment when he embarked on this wing.

He probably thought a fleeting thought again that immediately became reality. Still, as always – this trip is a unique pleasurable experience! Up here, in this infinite vastness, Rocco's longing quiets. Here, the irritating multiplicity of his life combines to a single, great, divine power of love.

"Where are we going this time?" the pearl eagle asks.

The Star Traveler

"No idea" says Rocco. He is so busy with the joy of his Being that he has no desire to arrive anywhere.

"You have an invitation" his soul whispers to him.

"Who wants to see me?" Rocco asks, astonished.

"Realize your heart's greatest desire and follow it!" his soul says. There, out of the deepest depth of his heart, a picture emerges. Rocco doesn't really want to take a closer look. His heart fears deception and disappointment. It fears that pain could be the price of joy.

"Forget your doubts and fears!" his reason suddenly interrupts. "Oh, you of all people should say something like that to me ... you who are usually the one who wants to x-ray everything with critical eyes ..."

"Well" his reason says. "This is fundamentally correct; but, if you do not follow the tracks of your deepest heart's desire, neither of us will live very long. Therefore, in this case I am acting from pure motivation for survival. Follow your heart's desire and stop plucking it apart. I promise I won't chastise you later for the consequences ..."

This promise dissolves Rocco's inhibitions. Thus, with great power, the picture of his heart's

The Star Traveler

desire unfolds within him: he sees, feels, hears and smells only one:

Clarina, the enchanting High Priestess of the planet Wega stands before him. She has appeared with a rushing sound. Rocco does not know if the rushing sound comes from his strongly vibrating blood stream, or from her wonderful silken garments. Her beauty halts his breath. His eagle has set him down softly on her planet. Now he stands here, twists his hands nervously, and his mouth gets dryer from second to second.

"You don't have to say anything" he hears Clarina speak within himself. Her voice, pure as a bell, seems to echo in each and every cell of his body.

"I see your colors and your light. I know what you feel!"

'How embarrassing' Rocco thinks, 'can one keep nothing to himself here?'

"There is also nothing to be embarrassed about" Clarina continues. "We have known and loved each other for a long time now. It is time to have an open conversation about it!"

The Star Traveler

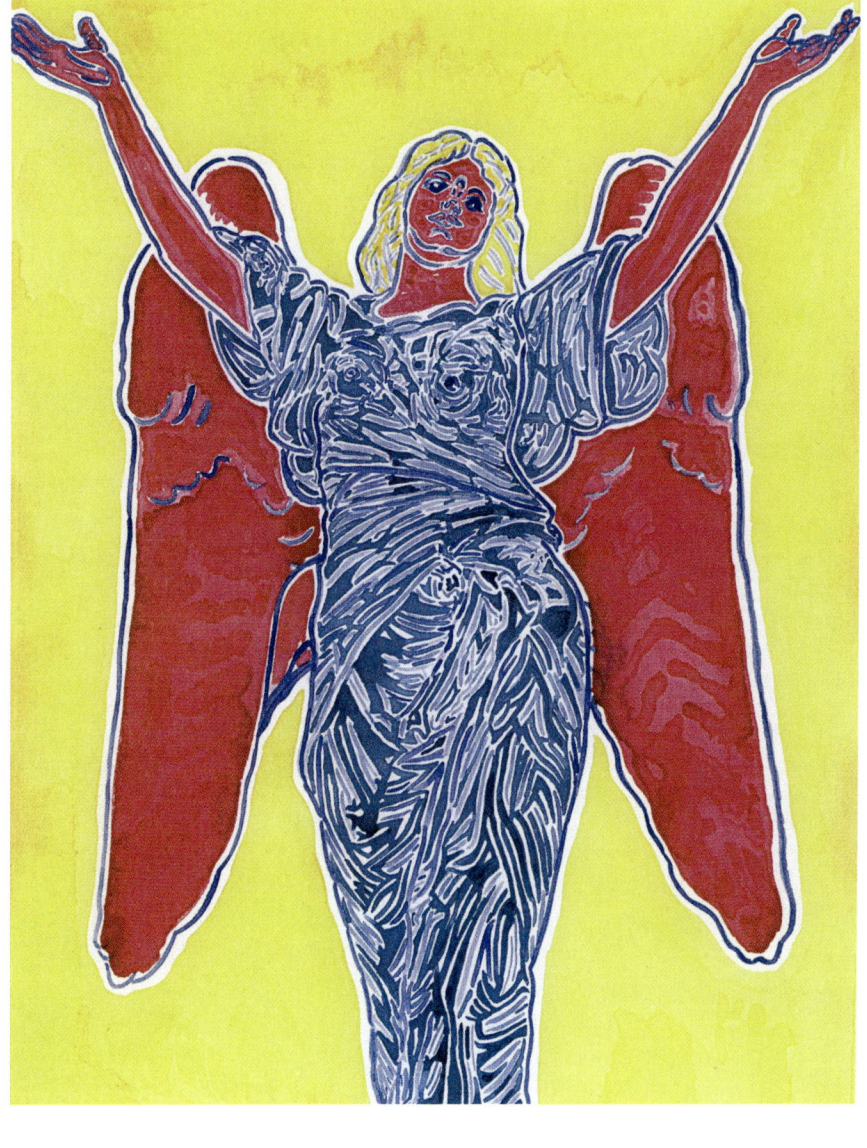

The Star Traveler

A hot tremor rushes through Rocco. Has she just said WE LOVE EACH OTHER? Could it be that

this wonderful fairy figure whom he has loved so endlessly long and deeply loves him?

"You know very well that I am not a fairy" she says now and again proves her ability to read his thoughts.

"I belong to the species of human angels. Inasmuch, we are perfectly compatible. If you, however, desire a life together with me, we will have to adjust our different frequencies to each other just a little. As soon as we begin to touch each other more often, this adjustment will happen all by itself."

Rocco trembles from head to toe. This woman actually steps into the core of all his secret desires and dreams. She stands blithely in the midst of his heart chamber.

"Well, this is my place, too! You called me here" she says quite happily.

'This could be a lot of fun …' Rocco thinks, and, filled with limitless joy in all his cells, sinks into her arms.

The Star Traveler

10

'Love is more natural and simpler than I ever imagined' he ponders, hours later. Together with Clarina, he lies upon a giant flowery meadow. Her planet, the sister planet Wega, vibrates in its especially fine, joyful love energy.

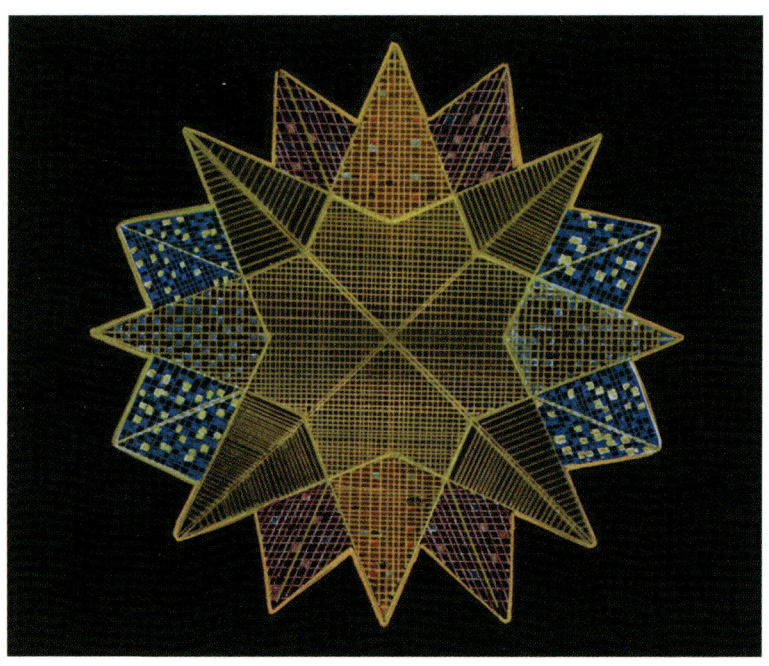

The planet has created a bed for them without compare in terms of preciousness. Finely scented, softly padded and, at the same time securely supportive, it offers a special foundation for their love. Its gravity is just a little less than earth's. Thus they seem to float while they rest, enfolded closely in each other's arms. 'Would my children like it here?' Rocco is just thinking. There - the deafening laughter and cheers of his class are already rolling over him.

"We told you we are already here!" Nina says. "As for your question: we think it's great to be here! This planet knows where it's at! Here, one can finally relax and enjoy life. When the planetary godhead is more evolved, the planet has a faster vibration; and then life for its inhabitants is much more beautiful and fun!"

Rocco is speechless. "How did you get here, all of you together?" he wants to know.
A storm of laughter answers him.
"Man, you ask questions …" Peter explodes with laughter. "You know how it works: we are fundamentally always everywhere! At home, at school, on this planet, on our way there, on other planets, in your heart, in the heart of your loved one, in the thoughts and feelings of our parents and siblings … when we want to be specifically 'present' somewhere, we just think about being there. We concentrate for a moment, bundle our energy and – poof – we're already here. Don't tell us you don't know this? You're doing the same thing?!"

The Star Traveler

Clarina has paid careful attention to the children. As she now looks into Rocco's dumbfounded face, she cannot control her laughter.

"It is only a matter of conscious awareness" Rocco hears her say. Somehow, his mind can take in no more. His head feels strangely empty. Rocco has no choice but to give up trying to understand.

11

Rocco wakes up from his own soft snoring. Something tickles him in a very intimate place. "This woman is a bit daring" he thinks.

"Not a bit – I am totally daring!" Clarina immediately answers, laughing.

"When you know for sure that your life is endless and you are always and totally loved, nothing remains to be feared! That means you can dare to do anything you want! However, I only want to do things that make me and others happy. When one knows that they are loved, they recognize the essence of love".

Automatically, Rocco looks around, trying to find the green dog. However, it is nowhere to be found. Only around Nina flows some of that mild, green light.

"Love spends itself" Clarina continues. "When one knows one is loved, one recognizes oneself as a work of art produced from purest love. Such a person is full of love. His acts are full of love."

"Pah – so much wisdom, and so early in the morning" Rocco thinks. Part of Clarina's speech, however, has drawn roots in him already. When one is sure of being loved, he automatically loves? Would that not be the ideal key to a peaceful co-existence on earth? What if all people could be sure of being loved?

"So, who should it be who loves them all?" his reason ventures somewhat disparagingly. "They are not all equally lovable?! Just think about all the rotten eggs and tyrants everywhere … so one creates sheer hell in another's life, and he should expect to be loved for it?"

In this moment, Rocco recognizes a breathtaking picture. It is so great and gorgeous that he doesn't even respond to his reason's arguments. He realizes – and all of his body's cells realize – the truth of the greater picture: Rocco now sees one giant human body. All of the cells in this body are made up of smaller bodies. All humans are a part of a greater organism. Each human is one part of a great human body.

Each takes on a personal mission within this great structure. Every one – really everyone! – of these missions is valuable for the fabric of life! A powerful, bright light streams through this whole human organism. Everywhere, it glitters and sparkles. Shimmering, in places phosphorescing, the stream of divine love energy lives, weaves, and moves through all realms of being. Each cell is filled with it.

"So, where does this light come from?" Rocco asks, amazed.

The Star Traveler

"Look down at your body" Clarina answers. There, Rocco realizes the level of miracle: brightly radiating light flows from the cells of his body. Glimmering, opalescent light nebulae penetrate and envelop him. He is ONE with all that lives around him. He feels only Oneness, levity, happiness, fulfillment, joy of life, self realization. Again, he recognizes the essence of love. Awe and gratitude fill him. The glow from his body grows stronger and stronger.

"Now you're almost as beautiful as your girlfriend" he hears a teasing voice behind him. Nina – the girl who allegedly cannot speak!
"Women are usually more beautiful than men" Nina continues unabashed. "They have less built-in boundaries. Therefore, more love light can flow through them. Admittedly, some of us ('us?' Rocco thinks – 'Nina isn't even a woman yet' … "girls and women have the same orientation. We all belong to the collective of women!" comes the prompt reply) – "so, many of us women have not yet discovered their natural beauty. They are always busy trying to make themselves beautiful; with make-up, clothes and all sorts of tricks. Most of them become less beautiful this way. The light has a hard time shining through all those layers. We women should love ourselves! Then the divine love light fills us and we are beautiful at once!"

"Well said, my Sweetie" says Clarina. "You girls are on the right track! Yes, you understood correctly: the female in us is mostly receiving. With our female qualities of surrender, lovingness, gentleness, and kindness, we open ourselves to receive the love light within us. Fundamentally, men can do this, too. Men, however, often let themselves be detoured by their reason. Women, too, block themselves through self hatred. Through thousands of years, we have created these patterns within ourselves. Yet, as of recently, a new energy exists that makes everything easier. The new love light is so fluid that it can even flow through stiffened patterns. In this process, it dissolves these softly. The only prerequisite for this is our desire!"

"I already have that" says Nina very seriously. "I have asked the divine spirit to renew me in his love light. Since then I have been changing constantly. I can do a lot of things that I could not do before: for instance speak. But, except for Rocco, nobody believes me. Even Rocco doubts sometimes and thinks he has misheard. When people have formed an opinion, it is hard to change their minds." Nina sounds almost a little sad in her observations.

The Star Traveler

Rocco decides to strengthen his faith in his perceptions in the future. Who cares about the medical diagnoses when life itself rewrites them?

12

A disconcerting thought shoots through Rocco's head: 'how late is it? What day is it? Shouldn't he be in school already?'

Like shiny glass, everything that had made him so happy shatters, in the blink of an eye. Clarina, their mutual love, the wonderful security on the planet Wega, and the many insights about the essence of love - everything hurries off and seems to leave him forever. "Noooo!" Rocco cries inside "Stay with me!!!!"

Still, he cannot prevent a terrible, frightening feeling of emptiness that spreads inside him. The more he tries to hold onto at least a part of this light, blissful happiness, the faster it flees from his consciousness.

"But, it should be possible to bring this living joy and lightness into the daily work" Rocco thinks on his way to school. "I cannot let it happen that I am crabby and irritated during the day and that my happy life begins at night in my sleep?"

"What you want you will have! What you decide happens" his soul whispers to him.

"That means that I am even to blame for this weary world?" Rocco asks, now really angry. There, from the midst of his heart, Clarina answers. Ah – how good it is to feel this energy! Immediately, warmth and brightness seeps into his body. She should always be with him; then everything would be easier …

"Please stop these thoughts of blame and innocence" he hears the bright voice of his Lover. "With this classification, you create more grief and stress in yourself. Humans create their world. All of you decide what sort of world you wish to live in. Expand your consciousness, and discover new possibilities for yourself this way! What if you nurtured this glowing lightness in your heart all day long? Every time a heavy thought wants to intrude, you exhale and let it go. Don't allow the heaviness to settle in. Well, what kind of a day would that be?"

"Real easy, of course" the green dog answers in Rocco's stead.

"Now where did HE come from again?" Rocco thinks, somewhat confused. Yet, his confusion no longer bothers him. With his next breath, he lets it go. So it comes that a beaming smile rides on his face as he enters school.

13

When Rocco comes home this evening, there is a letter on his threshold. The envelope gleams and glistens with a soft blue. "Who might have written to me?" Rocco thinks as he picks up the letter.
"Invitation to the initiation of the temple of sound" he reads a few moments later.

INVITATION TO THE INITIATION OF THE TEMPLE OF SOUND

The High Council of Sirius grants itself the honor to invite you to a special celebration! In the last 3,500 years, it has not been possible to create a healing temple of the universal life energy. The developments on planet Earth and her inhabitants have made it necessary for certain powerful tools to exist only in obscurity. As humanity had decided to undergo a time of separation from their own divine love energy, it would have been too dangerous to let it access these powerful tools.

We are now delighted to notify you that this necessary restriction has been lifted! Planet earth and her inhabitants have reached a new step in evolution. The magnetic field of divine

The Star Traveler

love energy is once more connected with humanity.

It will still take some time before all humans entirely understand the essence of their love energy and act accordingly. In order to further this evolutionary process, we of the High Council of Sirius, together with some of our earth siblings, have built the new cosmic temple of healing and sound. We will be delighted to personally introduce you to this wonderful, restorative place!

Together with you and additional guests, we will befittingly celebrate, for a whole week, a significant step in the history of mankind! Wonderful surprises await you! We extend a hearty welcome!

Respectfully and in the light of love, we remain

The High Council of Sirius

P.S. Your travel expenses to New Zealand and back will be reimbursed from a fund especially created for this purpose.

Rocco notices immediately that the date of the celebration falls within his vacation time. How

The Star Traveler

lucky! Or – is someone just playing a dumb joke on him?

"Someone is posing as an alien in order to get attention, and YOU promptly have to fall for it. Typical – you really are terribly naïve ..." he hears a familiar voice in the back ground. His reason has been quite peaceful for a while, but now it is fully active again.

"Look at the fine print; you'll surely find the hook" it sternly postulates.

"What if there isn't one this time?" Rocco tries timidly to defend his dream.

Suddenly, however, he realizes that this isn't necessary any more. His body vibrates with joy, and a soft glow permeates him. It almost feels as though he was embracing his beloved Clarina. All question marks and doubts flee from his cells and a wonderful feeling of love and hope remains. He will experience the initiation celebration of the sound temple! - although at this moment he has no clue about the next steps to lead him there.

"It works just so" his loving soul whispers to him. "Exactly this way you manifest things into existence: decide what you want to have or experience and enjoy them inside as though they were already happening. Yes, and leave the planning and issues of detail to the universe.

The Star Traveler

With your decision, you create a potentiality of power that must manifest, sooner or later. Matter follows thought!
It has no other choice, for it consists of thought made into form. The universe will provide everything– really everything! – You need in order to experience your thought in the form of matter. Your job is to find trust in the process. For every time you doubt the success of your plans, you squander energy from the account of your potentialities. You will get rapid results when you let this energy account work for you without disturbance!"

Rocco has listened intently to his soul. "If it is true that my thoughts become reality, why have some of my really important desires not yet come true?" he asks.
"You must be utterly clear and concentrated, dear Rocco" says his soul. "Only the concentrated attention of your whole Being has enough power to bring the objects of your desire into existence!
When you are scattered, you will receive scattered results. Most often you don't realize that these come into your life because of your scattered intent."
Rocco has a vague understanding of what his soul is trying to tell him here. He really hardly stays focused for long on his intent. Usually, at

some time, he begins to brood and doubt. Yes, it's true: in those moments he instantly stops feeling really powerful. "I'm going to New Zealand!" he decides therefore again with great clarity.

"And, in order for this plan to succeed, I will practice, from now on, giving all my attention, without doubt, to the success of this journey!"

"Wonderful – then we will be there together and celebrate" he hears Clarina say. Oh – this voice vibrates so sweetly in his cells that he instantly feels totally happy.

"Why don't we celebrate right now, already, and create an enchanting night together?" she asks him.

Did Rocco mishear, or did the voice come directly from within his bedroom? With a few steps he is there and can't believe his eyes: there is his girlfriend, more gleaming and beautiful than ever before, stretched out on his bed.

"How did you get here?" Rocco asks, happy and confused.

"But, you did wish for a night with me" Clarina says, blushing. "You did concentrate very keenly. The arrow of your attention and intention has hit its mark. So I caught it, and hence I am here!"

Rocco is too happy to care how this new miracle could happen for him. Full of bliss, excitement and joy, he lets himself fall onto the bed and embraces his dearly beloved.

The Star Traveler

14

Are human women as affectionate and gentle as his mate from Wega? So far, Rocco has never had such an intense intimate encounter with a woman. Clarina is the most beautiful one for him, and far ahead of the race. He cannot at all imagine being even half as happy with any other woman.

"You don't have to be, either" says Clarina and tickles his back.

"I am quite content to be your choice. We really could stay together forever!"

Rocco sighs with longing. Oh, that would be great … but he has no idea how this is possible …

"Have you already forgotten what you have learned about your desires, matter and reality?" Clarina now asks very seriously.

"Concentrate on your wish and stop this brooding. Leave the work of manifestation to the universe. That is much more practical, anyway, don't you think? Just let creation work for you and surrender to the development!"

While she says this, she smiles impishly. She looks so sweet that Rocco must kiss her deeply –right now. Does she have any idea how they can create their future together? ….

"Hush – I'm not telling!" she says, laughingly and puts her finger on his lips.

"Seductress" Rocco thinks and embraces her even more passionately.

"Just take me to school with you. The children will certainly enjoy it" Clarina says the next morning.
"And how will I explain this to the dean?" Rocco's reason asks broodingly.
'I really don't care' Rocco thinks suddenly.
He gets up, takes his beloved by the hand and happily gets underway with her. This will definitely be a fun day at school!

15

What a wonderful night his beloved has given him! Rocco is still filled with her warmth and tenderness. Clarina sits next to him on the bus, and the whole world seems to glow. Although it is raining again profusely, Rocco feels a wonderful lightness.
"I am reaching my goals! I will be there in New Zealand with Clarina!" he thinks with a jubilant heart.

Even the gray school building seems to glow today. As they step into the big foyer, it smells like … well, like what? Usually one can hardly breathe in here. Wet raincoats, sweaty sports uniforms, stale cigarette smoke (even though that shouldn't be possible because the school is a no smoking zone…), stale lunch sandwiches. Like a cloud, the daily effluvium of a hundred people descends upon everyone who enters this building. Today, however, a fresh breeze is mingled into all that. The whole atmosphere in the school has been altered by it.
'What is this?' Rocco thinks. 'The scent of blossoms? A salty scent of the ocean? Fresh, green meadows …? New Zealand!' the thought rushes through him. How can this be though? Rocco looks at Clarina. Has she noticed it also?

The Star Traveler

"Your thoughts are taking form" his soul whispers. Curious about what else he might experience, he opens the class room door.

All the children are sitting in their places and smiling peacefully to themselves. Even here in the class room Rocco notices the fresh breeze of blossoms, ocean and meadow. It is strangely quiet, too …. Only now Rocco becomes aware that this has never happened before. Usually, when he enters class in the morning, he must first try to get some attention in the midst of loud laughter and shouting. Now this quiet … all the children are looking at Clarina with expectation.

"Are you lovers now?" Peter asks finally. As Clarina nods, beaming, all the children clap their hands. Rocco is much moved. It seems as though his handicapped children are extending a special blessing to him and the woman he loves. Quite apparently, they are delighted about his union with her.
"Now everything will be new!" he hears a small boy say thoughtfully.
Then the mild green light of true love energy glows along with the fresh meadow scent in the class. Rocco feels deeply relaxed and oddly lost in reverie.

The Star Traveler

"New Zealand is everywhere" Nina says, seriously now. "But, since it is so wonderful, we will still go there during vacation!"
She adds laughingly.
"You want to go to New Zealand?" the question escapes from Rocco. "What do you want to do there? Are you all going together?"
Now, the children are a bit embarrassed. What are they hiding from him?
"We cannot tell you yet", an older boy interjects. "It has to do with a few surprises we are preparing for you and the other guests at the initiation". – So they know about the invitation to the temple initiation? Strange – what else is happening behind his back? Rocco wonders to himself.
"Yes, we are all going together. Some are even bringing their parents and siblings. And, a delegation from Sirius will accompany us. Other kids, from other countries, are coming, too!"

Rocco can only marvel. How much his inner and outer world has changed in the last few months! His school children are planning a trip! A few weeks ago, they were still thought of as handicapped and were taken care of all day long. Now they are speaking confidently about their ideas and plans. Have their parents and siblings noticed how much they are growing? He will have to let the dean know in detail.

The Star Traveler

"To be Self-cognizant means to know the truth about our inner potentialities" Clarina whispers softly to him. "Those are, as we know, limitless!" "Well, then let us enjoy a happy day of school together" Rocco says to the children. While they unpack books and journals, a humming atmosphere of fun and business weaves through the class room.

16

In the evening, Clarina takes her leave of him. Rocco finds it more and more unbearable to be without her. Still, this time even his silent, bitter cry is of no avail; she must go. Although she may prefer to stay herself, her tasks as High Priestess on Wega are calling her. So, Rocco returns alone to his empty apartment. It seems dark and cold. The lamps he lights cannot dissipate this darkness. All his familiar furnishings have a strange, dull and disturbing effect on him.

"I could easily give all this up" he thinks for a fleeting moment.

Immediately, he stands in the midst of a blooming, warm landscape. All around him is bright sunlight. A creek murmurs and ripples at his side. Nature glows and shines in innumerable, soft pastel colors. Intoxicating flower scents fill his nose.

"Where have I landed now?" Rocco asks.

"When you give something up, the door to the realms of your desires opens!" Rocco hears his beloved star master say.

"Oh dear – perhaps I was a little hasty here …" Rocco thinks. "Can I never return to my apartment? Have I really given it up forever?" he

asks of the star master. "I must return to my school children ..."
"These you will find everywhere" answers the Sirian quietly. "The children and you – and many others – you are in service together. You will visit many other places to serve."

Even as Rocco holds the great star master's great wisdom in high esteem, he finds these words confusing. Again and again, his familiar image of the world is turned around. Even a few months ago, everything seemed so clear: he was a teacher of handicapped children. At night, he dreamed of wonderful galaxies far away. Every morning, he found himself again in the normal world. Often he felt dissatisfied and bored. At least, however, there was a certain order to life that he could trust.

And now? Everything that seemed right has dissolved. His school children have developed new skills. In an eerie way, they often seem to understand more than he does; and he could gain many an insight through them while he himself, helpless and amazed, discovered new realms of life. Where would all this lead him eventually? Rocco feels very insecure. In this moment, he is not so sure that his constant desire for travel hasn't gone too far. Still, he is

The Star Traveler

standing in this wonderful, softly glowing landscape.

"Just enjoy being here and leave the brooding alone …" his soul whispers to him.

"Right" Rocco thinks and takes a deep breath. Something comes bounding towards him across the meadow. Is he deceiving himself, or can he hear the laughter of his children? Before he can think, a funny colorful monkey stands next to him, and happiness fills his heart. "I'll leave you two alone" he hears the star master say. The monkey takes him by the hand and, with pizzazz, romps around the meadow with him.

Since his childhood, Rocco has not been so breathless. He had forgotten how much fun it was to be so frisky. Now, however, his body needed a break. Laughing and puffing he lets himself fall onto the grass while the monkey still dances around him and turns one somersault after the other. "Carefree life" Rocco thinks … - how long has it been since he felt so free?
"Exactly this is what all people may learn again now" the monkey says, and bows with a hop, like a clown. "And, when you start, other will soon join in" he adds. "This is why we all celebrate in New Zealand!"

The Star Traveler

"What - you, too?" Rocco asks, still out of breath. "So this will be meeting of all sorts of beings …? Why must it happen implicitly in New

Zealand?" The monkey looks at Rocco strangely for a moment.

'Funny' Rocco thinks – 'sometimes his face looks like a dog …'

"You really don't know?" asks the monkey.

As Rocco shakes his head no, he sighs a little.

"You humans really still need frequent tutoring. The children are more advanced, but you adults … I thought for sure you would know since you have such a good connection with the star master ...ok – then listen:

New Zealand has always been a special place on your planet. Some of you have realized this and made a beautiful movie there a few years ago. In this movie, you can see many things most of you have already totally forgotten. Magic, nature spirits, elves, the power of the trees and plants – New Zealand lies on a light ray from Sirius. Your earth loves to receive the white/blue rays of Sirius' sun immensely. This special ray power permeates it and nourishes its fire. You know that there are big volcanoes on New Zealand. That is where the star portals are located that connect humanity with other regions of the universe.

On the light ray from Sirius, special energies come to you humans. They further your development. There are other places on earth where such things happen as well. New Zealand, however, is specially equipped to

The Star Traveler

enable a meeting of diverse beings and worlds. Moreover, it has a well-built landing place for UFOs. So, now you know why we celebrate in New Zealand!"

After this long speech, the monkey seems to need exercise. Immediately, he begins again with his constant frisky jumps and somersaults. "New Zealand's worth the traveled miles" he sings and thrills without pause. "Everyone will be there, and a new era begins!"
Rocco has so many thoughts in his head at the same time that he gets tired.
"What will happen with my apartment?" he asks the monkey. That one, however, cannot be bothered with such a worldly practical problem. "Everything in its own good time …" he sings and turns circles and figure eights until Rocco gets dizzy just from watching and must close his eyes.

17

Rocco finds it great to be traveling as an adventurer, but a little more rest and harmony than he has experienced lately would be nice. Just now he lies on the sunny meadow and feels really relaxed again after a long time. While the monkey is still jumping and dancing around, Rocco has gotten comfortable. Simply to be here, to stretch out, to loll, to send reason on a vacation – how wonderful it is to feel so supported! The planet on which he rests fills his body with a very special energy. Something permeates him, strengthens him and warms him through and through. From minute to minute he feels quieter and happier.

"Where might I be" he asks the jumping dancing monkey after a while.
"Well, I'll be – where is your intuition?" the monkey complains. "We've been talking about it the whole time and you still haven't gotten it? On New Zealand, of course! Right smack within the love light ray of Sirius' suns!"
Suddenly, Rocco is wide awake. This here is New Zealand? How did he travel here?
"The impulse of your intent was strong enough to make you change location" he hears a familiar –oh so dearly beloved voice.

Before him, in the bright sunlight, stands Clarina. She is wrapped in coral red silken scarves that make the light play secretively on her skin, making her so beautiful that Rocco is speechless. The wind is playing with her hair, and golden rays flow everywhere around her. His Beloved! Rocco can hardly grasp his fortune. She is here! A golden stream of unconditional love flows from her eyes to him – right into the middle of his heart. In this moment, all his doubts and brooding thoughts are dissolved.

"The dissolving of all doubts means salvation!" she says now, laughing. How sweet the sound of her voice …Naturally she knows exactly what is happening inside him.
"Of course I know it" she says now. "Have you still not understood that we are of the same kind? We live in the same energy field! Actually, this is true for all humans, but most are entirely unaware of it. Those who are united in love, however, feel it right away, this field. This is how all things in life become simpler, easier. When you realize how intimately connected you are with all that is, you can relax and let your soul dangle!"

'Maybe I really don't want to be connected with everyone?' Rocco thinks as memories of particularly unpleasant neighbors rise up in him. 'There are people I really want nothing to do with, otherwise I'd constantly be angry …'

His beloved has reclined on the sweetly scented grass and gently caresses his hair. Rocco looks into her eyes and seems to drown in them. It feels like he is traveling through the infinite, glimmering stars …

"A glimmering universe in every one of us …" his soul whispers softly, and a happy tremor flows through Rocco from head to toe.

"As long as you reject even one human from inside, you reject yourself" Clarina says, seriously. "If you don't like your neighbor, look again closely and discover his glowing soul. It lives in every human regardless how he acts. Do not let him anger you. Do not anger yourself. You create anger within you. You can just as well leave it be"

Rocco feels a little hurt. He does not like school-like lectures. Pouting, he retreats into his shell. Clarina's gentle voice, however, allows him to soften again right away:

"There is a secret in the recognition of divinity. Recognize the divine in all representations of your world and be whole!"

Oh Dear – another chunk of philosophy. Rocco does not feel like thinking any more. He enjoys Clarina's soft hands on his body. Happily he enfolds her in his arms and leaves "being

The Star Traveler

whole" or "being half" to those who absolutely want to know. While his thoughts dissipate in the sun light, Rocco actually feels perfectly and wonderfully whole.

18

Hours later, he wakes in Clarina's arms. It is night, and the velvet blue sky stretches over them like a dome.

'Just like in a four-poster bed, we rest here' Rocco ponders. While his spirit dives into the infinite vastness, it is as though thousands of gleaming star patterns are flowing toward him. Each light gives him a very special quality. Rocco feels how his consciousness again expands to make room for this abundance. More and more facets of the heavenly light spread inside him, and suddenly he understands what it means to be whole.

"This is how you become a star master!" his soul whisper very softly in him. Its gentle voice seems to come from everywhere. Each and every one of his cells moves with its sound. Rocco feels how it pours itself out – within and without – are there even any limits for the many different realms of his being left?

The most delicate violet and rose now spreads across the sky at the horizon. From the edge of the woods, the first voices of the birds herald the morning. First just a few cautious little sounds – as though the little feathered maestros of the skies were practicing themselves into the day. After just a few moments, they are already tuned in and fill this wonderful morning with their concert. Rocco feels Clarina move and stretch in his arms. She blinks a little, and then a beaming smile covers her whole face.

"You are gorgeous, my Dearest" Rocco whispers in her ear and kisses her full of passion. Clarina looks at him attentively, and suddenly her eyes get really big in amazement.

"Wow" she exclaims – "the light flows in you! You have become a star master!"

Her carefree, joyous cheer mixes in with the concert of thousands of bird voices.

"Now we can marry" she says after a few minutes, happy and determined.

'What practical thinkers women are …' her Beloved thinks to himself.

The Star Traveler

19

They must have dozed off for a little nap: a gleaming bright sun shines down on them when they open their eyes again. The rays of the sun are tickling them everywhere
"Well, let's go!" Rocco says and jumps up. "I could eat a horse!" Hand in hand with Clarina, he bounces over the shiny meadow.
Soon, their path ends at a gentle downward slope. Wide plains stretch beneath them: flowers, meadows, creeks, corn fields and forests as far as the eye can see. Far in the distance, snow covered mountain giants climb up into the heavens. At the foothills, something glimmers and glitters in the sunlight. Rocco and Clarina blink to make out more clearly what it is. Even before their eyes can understand, however, what they see, they both know simultaneously that they have discovered another destination in their travels.
Clarina beams at her Beloved. "Let us be there right away" he hears her voice in his heart. In the same moment they are standing, full of awe, before the new healing temple of the new age.

Without a doubt this is the most beautiful building they have ever seen! Like a giant flower it stands before them. Infinitely tall is its construct. Rocco cannot at all understand what sort of building materials could create such a spectacle; and a spectacle it is, this temple. For, while they are contemplating it, it constantly changes its appearance.

"Nothing remains as it is" Rocco thinks and remembers the many hours of teaching from his Master. "Everything is in constant motion"

Transparent glimmering walls (or is it windows?) stretch out like round domes in all directions. Opalescent and fluorescent colors flow over these curvatures – or are the domes and curvatures themselves moving? Impossible to say which is real.

"Just like in real life" he hears a happy voice. Nina is here! All the children of his class are standing around her.

Rocco's mind turns a little somersault: 'How can the children stand? What happened to their wheelchairs?'

Yet, in all this turbulence, he remains without an answer. In the background, Rocco also notices some of the children's parents. They are standing together, somewhat embarrassed.

"Boy, you have changed!" Peter erupts. "You got real bright! Have you really managed to stop all the brooding and doubts?"

"When you have the right woman, everything gets much easier" cries Nina with a glance at

Peter, and giggles with enthusiasm. She seems to blush slightly …

Does Rocco delude himself, or has he just seen a couple of bright red, sparking waves between the two?

"Now we'll really have a big celebration" another girl says excitedly.

Then, as though something had called them all at once, the children flow, laughing and chatting, through the gates into the building.

Just now Rocco notices the sounds. Surprised, he listens more closely as Clarina observes him with a smirk. "Right, Rocco" he hears her say "Everything is sound. All manifestations are created from a harmony of different sounds. You could also say that the world consists of a composition of different frequencies. Sounds or colors make up the movable patterns of different velocity and proportion. The denser these sound patterns become, the better you can understand them as matter. This temple was created in order to remind humanity of its original Being. Colors and sounds will accompany us now as long as we are here."

Rocco marvels. How does his Beloved know all these things? Somehow she seems often to be ahead of him by a few steps. Reluctantly Rocco admits to himself how much she always surprises him.

"Forget your vanity" his soul whispers inside him. "Just relax and discover the same wisdom within yourself! Do you still remember how she told you that you were of the same kind? 'Right' Rocco thinks. In a flash, he knows that he also knows.

"Let's go in! I am so eager to know what expects us here" he says, puts his arm around Clarina and enters the temple with her.

Mauve light receives them in the interior. Just as Rocco excitedly observes the play of color on Clarina's skin, everything already looks different. Surrounded by deep blue rays, they continue their path. Colors and sounds envelop them, and everything is constantly changing. Then they enter a dome shaped ruby-red room. This must be the reception, for numerous very small different Beings seem to wait for something. His school children, too, are in the crowd. Oh, and - there! – in the back is the green dog, totally immersed in a conversation with the funny monkey. Somehow the monkey is able to turn somersaults even in the middle of a conversation.

In one corner, Rocco recognizes the delegation of the Sirians. They are having a conversation with some of the parents of his class. Rocco has

The Star Traveler

never seen the parents so relaxed and happy. He would surely like to know what is being discussed there … However; telepathic connections are apparently only made when all are in agreement?

An immensely beautiful woman now approaches and welcomes them.

"My name is Iriana" she says by way of introduction. "We are delighted that you are here. Would you like to celebrate your wedding with us these days?" Rocco sees his Beloved blush slightly.

'How did this make the rounds so quickly?' he thinks. 'Did Clarina …' but she looks deep into his eyes and resolutely shakes her head no.

"Will you finally grasp the consequences of Being One!" she whispers to him. "I don't have to spread any words at all. Whoever is awake, understands anyway what is happening …"

"Yes, of course, so it is" adds Iriana, smiling. "Nothing about this has to be uncomfortable for you. We all live in the field of love where the usual boundaries may fall. Laws of embarrassment or private safe zones are only necessary where we are not sure of love. This is the place where we can all remember our collective source, and because of this we may know what moves each other."

The Star Traveler

While these words were spoken, the whole room seemed filled with gentle green light, and Rocco could finally understand the message from the green dog.

20

"Do you know what purpose this temple will fulfill in the future?" Rocco asks Clarina as they arrive in their personal resting room later.
"It serves for healing. Healing happens from remembrance" Clarina answers.
"Remembrance means: to go within. Inside ourselves, we find everything – really everything! – we need for a happy life! Whosoever, in the future, wants to, can remember in this temple what a wonderful light dwells within him. The builders of the temple have created a very special force field here. Sounds, colors and magnetic fields stimulate the bodily cells of its visitors. This is how movement begins in the cell's memory. Within the light patterns of the human body, all information is saved. The tissue remembers and healing becomes possible."

While he listens to his Beloved, Rocco's gaze wanders around the room. Upon their arrival he first noticed the fresh scent of roses and took a few delicious deep breaths. Colors of a rosy hue fill every corner of the room. This welcome message changed, however, after only a short while. Royal blue light is enveloping them now. Rocco feels very quiet and deeply relaxed. His body is pleasantly warm, and his thoughts are

The Star Traveler

drifting. Suddenly, the borders of the room seem to dissipate, and Rocco recognizes the ray of light that flows from here to the farthest regions of the universe. Wait – should this ray not come down to earth from Sirius? Rocco watches his Beloved and knows exactly what she would say: All is ONE! The different directions of the love light, too, are fundamentally ONE. Really important is only that these rays connect everything with everything!

"Colors and sounds build the essence of life. Magnetic love light holds all of it in its form" his soul whispers deep inside him. "You know the secret now, Rocco. With that, you are ready for a new round!"

The Star Traveler

The Star Traveler

21

After a magical, refreshing night, Rocco wakes up in the arms of his Beloved. Golden light fills their shared space. A deep, calm sound – like that of a well cast bell – hovers over them. From outside, the many-voiced bird concert of a sunny morning pours into the room. Today will be their wedding, and at the same time, the temple will be initiated; the temple that from now on will be available to all who want to realize the joy of their lives. Rocco's mood is very solemn. The day before, he was allowed, together with Clarina, to participate in a gathering of the Council of Sirius. Both of them learned many interesting things about their future tasks and paths. Rocco is immensely delighted with their future shared life. Even just a while ago, he had not dared dream what is now already reality. Deep inside him, something giggles
"So dream more daringly from now on! You can see that it pays off …" he hears his soul twitter.
His time as school teacher is now forever over. For even his children will take over special tasks. He still knows little about them, only that they will, together with the children of other countries, be something like diplomats. Diplomats of a new age in which adults are ready to learn from children …

The Star Traveler

Rocco lolls and yawns profusely. His wonderful lover sighs softly in her sleep and cuddles closely to him. His heart drums an extra beat out of sheer joy.

Yesterday, something entirely surprising happened to him during the gathering of the Sirians. Amongst the various guests of honor from the most different regions of the universe, Rocco suddenly discovered his school inspector. The woman against whom the dean had warned him! Greatly shocked, he initially tried to make himself as invisible as possible, but apparently he had failed, because during a break, she came directly to him. Quickly then, he found that his worries were absolutely unnecessary. Now Rocco knows that even in the school administration, there are people who are working on new solutions for friendly schools. Today, his school inspector will even have a sort of counseling session with his children. In his mind, Rocco hears his dean laugh out loud as he realizes that business and fun are two aspects of the same experience.

Clarina has woken up and kisses Rocco very gently on the tip of his nose.

"Good Morning, my husband-to-be" she whispers in his ear. "I am SO looking forward to marrying you! Wega is a love planet. For quite some time, she has longed for a union with

The Star Traveler

Earth. Now she can finally rejoice over the sparkling union of these energies!"
While Clarina hugs him friskily and passionately, Rocco senses how many different meanings her words possess. Filled with grateful joy, he returns her embrace. Crimson light enfolds them both while they experience the truth:

All is One – here – now! And love holds within itself the greatest of all miracles!

The Star Traveler

Rocco's Story and our Thanks!

Our warmest thanks to you, Dear Reader, for your interest in Rocco and life's multi-layered dimensions! The world and all the life therein are wonderful and precious to us; and we rejoice in everyone who is attracted to our joy this way.

Rocco announced his appearance within us as early as seven years ago. At that time, the gentle voices of our intuition whispered thoughts and images about his life. It was only in this past year, however, that we could draw these images and write the story. As in the time before the birth of a child, we had to be patient; for somehow, this special energy had not yet been released. When finally the text and the images developed, we fervently asked within our selves to find an appropriate publisher for this book. And, before we could blink an eye, our dear friend Marita Mitschein volunteered for the project.

Marita found our translator, Roselle Nordtome, who immediately understood the deeper meaning of the story and expressed it in English. Thank you so much, dear Roselle, for this fine work! We know that you have done

The Star Traveler

much more than just translate. It takes not only excellent language skills but also literary talent to transfer these layers of meaning into another language.

To you, dear Marita Mitschein, we extend our warmest thanks for your truly outstanding competence and your compassionate dedication to this book! We could not have found a better publisher! With you, Rocco and his issues (which are really all of our issues) are in the best hands! It is a pleasure working with you!

Our deepest thanks also to the multiform of our heavenly helpers in visible and invisible form! We listen, dear Ones, and experience with deep gratitude the security and care you grant us in every moment of our lives!

We greet you light-heartedly, with love, and gratitude!

Yours,

Dr. Ilse-Maria and Jürgen Fahrnow

About the Authors

Dr. Ilse-Maria Fahrnow, M.D., is a medical doctor and psychologist. In her 10-year practice at SOS-Kinderdorf e.V. and 15 years in her own practice, she has gathered extensive experience in working with people.

Photograph by Jan Röder

Dr. Fahrnow, together with her husband, Jürgen Fahrnow, now lives and practices energy healing and channeling in Munich, Germany.

Jürgen Fahrnow is a certified Rolfer and energy healer. He uses his artistic talents to create pictograms, symbols and pictures that facilitate healing. Dr. Ilse-Maria and Jürgen Fahrnow together also facilitate workshops for light and earth healing in which they share their multi-layered knowledge and energies.

Web site of Dr. Ilse-Maria und Jürgen Fahrnow:
www.alleelemente.de

Web site of SOS Kinderdorf e.V.:
www.sos-childrensvillages.org

The Star Traveler

Previous publications by the authors:

➢ Feng Shui in the kitchen, co-authored with Guenther Sator, Graefe & Unzer, Munich, 1999; English version at Gaia Books Ltc., 2002

➢ Feng Shui and the 5-element kitchen, co-authored with Guenther Sator, Graefe und Unzer, Munich, 2000; American version at Silverback Books Inc., 2000

➢ Five Element Nutrition, Graefe & Unzer, Munich, complete revised and expanded new edition 2005

➢ Jin Shin Jyutsu – practical exercises, Knaur, Munich, 2002

➢ The Healing Power of Your Hands – self help with Jin Shin Jyutsu, Knaur, Munich, 2004

➢ The Goddess in the New Millennium, ch.falk-verlag, Seeon, 2006